Fox in a Box

Illustrated by The Artful Doodlers

Random House 🏠 New York
Thomas the Tank Engine & Friends™

CREATED BY BRITT ALLCROFT

Based on The Railway Series by The Reverend W Awdry. © 2010 Gullane (Thomas) LLC.
Thomas the Tank Engine & Friends and Thomas & Friends are trademarks of Gullane (Thomas) Limited.
HIT and the HIT Entertainment logo are trademarks of HIT Entertainment Limited.
All rights reserved. Published in the United States by Random House Children's Books, a division of Random House, Inc., 1745 Broadway, New York, NY 10019, and in Canada by Random House of Canada Limited, Toronto. Step into Reading, Random House, and the Random House colophon are registered trademarks of Random House, Inc.
www.stepintoreading.com   www.randomhouse.com/kids   www.thomasandfriends.com

Educators and librarians, for a variety of teaching tools, visit us at
www.randomhouse.com/teachers
ISBN: 978-0-375-85368-5   MANUFACTURED IN CHINA

HiT entertainment

Thomas and Percy want
to have a party!
They have a big kit in a box.
The kit has some nuts,
bags, and caps.

Look!

It is a fox.

It is a bad fox.

"The fox is in the box!"

says Thomas.

"He wants some nuts,"

says Percy.

The fox nips and rips the bags.

"Where is Driver Dan?"

says Thomas.

"Driver Dan will get the fox."

Rain!

It is raining.

The fox runs and hides.

The fox likes nuts, not rain.

A big box.

The fox hid in that big box.

The fox wants the sun.

Where is the fox?

The fox is in the big box.

The fox can not

nip and rip the bags.

Thomas and Percy can have fun!

The party is fun.

But not for the fox.